SLIP JIG SUMMER

Elizabeth J.M. Walker

ORCA BOOK PUBLISHERS

Library and Archives Canada Cataloguing in Publication

Walker, Elizabeth J. M., 1983–, author
Slip jig summer / Elizabeth J.M. Walker.
(Orca limelights)

Issued in print and electronic formats.
ISBN 978-1-4598-1743-2 (softcover).—ISBN 978-1-4598-1744-9 (pdf).—
ISBN 978-1-4598-1745-6 (epub)

I. Title. II. Series: Orca limelights
PS8645 A45965 S55 2018   JC813'.6   C2017-904564-4
C2017-904565-2

First published in the United States, 2018
Library of Congress Control Number: 2017949705

Summary: In this high-interest novel for teen readers, ballet-obsessed
Natalie has to spend the summer with her Irish-dancing cousins.

*Orca Book wPublishers is dedicated to preserving the environment and has printed
this book on Forest Stewardship Council® certified paper.*

Orca Book Publishers gratefully acknowledges the support for
its publishing programs provided by the following agencies:
the Government of Canada through the Canada Book Fund and the Canada
Council for the Arts, and the Province of British Columbia through the
BC Arts Council and the Book Publishing Tax Credit.

Cover photography by Shutterstock.com/urbazon
Edited by Tanya Trafford

ORCA BOOK PUBLISHERS
www.orcabook.com

Printed and bound in Canada.

21 20 19 18 • 4 3 2 1

For Mom and Dad

One

"Has anyone seen my lipstick?" Yumi asked, frantically searching the dressing room's counter.

"You mean this one?" Amber asked as she applied a bright red layer to her lips.

Yumi scowled and held out her palm. "Hand it over."

"How do you *still* not have your own stage makeup?" I asked. I was sitting on the floor doing up my pointe-shoe ribbons.

"Because I know I can borrow everything from the two of you?" Amber said. She pinned once last loose piece of hair into her bun. "Right, Natalie? Can I borrow your blush?"

I sighed. "It's in my makeup bag."

Amber smiled as she picked up my pink polka-dot bag and rifled through. I didn't mind. The three of us had been dancing together for the past five years—since we were ten. We were prepping for our annual year-end ballet recital.

"Two minutes!" the stage manager called over the intercom.

"Was that for us?" Amber asked.

"Yes!" Yumi said. "Hurry up and finish your makeup."

I stood and looked in the mirror to make sure I didn't have any stray hair poking out of my bun. I smoothed out the front of my purple-satin bodysuit. Amber reached over and fluffed up the long purple tutu.

"I love these costumes," Yumi said, looking at herself in the mirror. "I can't believe we're finally dancing 'Waltz of the Flowers.'"

I smiled at her reflection. "We earned it."

"Waltz of the Flowers" is a dance from the ballet *The Nutcracker*, but one that isn't considered too Christmasy. It was performed every year at the recital, and it was always the first dance a class would perform on pointe. The part of Dewdrop was performed by one of the more experienced dancers at the school.

"One minute!" the stage manager announced.

"We have to go!" I said to Amber. She was adding some finishing touches to her eye makeup.

"I know, I know!" Amber said but didn't budge from the mirror.

"Amber! Put the eyeliner down!" Yumi said and started shoving Amber toward the door.

We were in one of the smaller, older theaters in Toronto. There were two levels of dressing rooms backstage, all connected by narrow hallways. We passed other dancers on our way to the stage door: little kids in pink tutus, older dancers in feathery Swan costumes. We met up with the rest of the girls from our class.

"Pinkies!" I whispered and held up my pinkie finger. I shook pinkies with Amber, Yumi and the rest of my class for good luck before heading through the stage door.

We had to wait quietly in the wings while the soloist on stage, one of the senior dancers, finished her "Dying Swan" solo from *Swan Lake*. I got goose bumps on my arms as she danced—

it was so beautiful. The crowd applauded as she took her final curtsey and the red velvet curtain came down.

It was our class's turn. We got into position in our opening V-formation—with Amber and I at the tip of the V since we were the tallest. The curtain rose. The music began, and we danced. There wasn't anything else quite like dancing onstage— the lights, the adrenaline making my turns crisper, my kicks higher. I loved the sound of our pointe shoes as we landed a jump in unison, the rustle of our tutus as we moved about the stage.

It was always over much too soon. We hit our final pose: arabesques around Dewdrop. The audience applauded as Dewdrop curtseyed, and then we Flowers took our own curtsey. The curtain came down, and I sighed as I left the magic of the stage behind.

Two

We still had one more dance to perform. We changed out of our purple flower costumes and into much simpler costumes—navy-blue leotards with matching wrap skirts. Our second dance was a more modern dance our teacher, Michelle, had choreographed. It was set to an upbeat violin piece by Lindsey Sterling.

"Uck," Yumi said as she patted her forehead with tissues. "Why must dancing require so much sweating?"

"Dancers do not sweat—we *perspire!*" Amber said as she blotted her own forehead.

"Here," I said as I rooted around in my makeup bag. "I have some *actual* blotting papers. No need to use up the dressing room's entire supply of tissues."

"You're always so prepared, Natalie!" Amber said. "Oh, and I might need to use your finishing powder again too."

"Of course," I said, laughing.

"You're both taking summer classes, right?" Yumi asked as she began sticking a couple more bobby pins into her bun.

Amber and I exchanged looks in the mirror. "Of course!" we both said.

"Only *novices* take summers off," Amber said haughtily.

While we waited for our next dance, we stretched to keep our bodies warm and chatted— about boys at our schools (we all went to different high schools), what dances we might get to do the next year (I was dying to do the "Dance of the Swans" from *Swan Lake*), and who might be teaching the summer session (sometimes it was Michelle, and sometimes it was a much sterner teacher named Madame Lebrun, who we often called Madame No Fun).

"One minute until 'Beyond the Veil,'" announced the stage manager.

"That's us!" Amber said. "Let's make Michelle proud."

Yumi nodded. "I love this dance."

"Me too." I did a last check in the mirror before I left our dressing room.

This time we were following one of the pre-school classes dancing to "The Teddy Bears' Picnic." They wore fluffy white tutus and each held a stuffed bear. It was pretty adorable.

The curtain came down. Yumi, Amber and I went onstage first. The rest of the class joined in throughout the piece, and all of us did one big combination together. Then we quickly exited, each of us doing a different turn or leap. I danced off doing a series of piqué turns. I lost my balance and nearly fell into Yumi, who was doing a grande jeté.

"Yikes, close one," Yumi whispered once we were in the wings.

"Sorry," I whispered back and felt my face flush. I would definitely be working on my piqué turns over the summer.

We headed back to our dressing room, dripping sweat once more. I handed out the blotting papers. Yumi also wiped off her bright red lipstick.

"Yuck, I can't stand stage makeup," she said.

I wiped off my lipstick too. It always felt tacky and gross, no matter what lip gloss I tried to smooth over top of it. Amber touched hers up.

"I like it," she said, admiring her made-up face in the mirror.

"If you like it so much, maybe you should bring your own next year," Yumi said.

Amber changed the subject. "Did your dad come this year?" she asked me.

"Ha, as if," I said. "He's still traveling the world. I got a birthday card from China a while ago. And last year it was New Zealand."

"Sorry," Yumi said.

"Maybe next year," Amber said.

"I doubt it," I told them. My parents split when I was two. It's just me and my mom at home, but I don't mind. She works a lot but always finds time to drive me to my ballet classes. She says watching me do something I'm so passionate about makes it all worth it.

I changed into my after-show outfit—a blue sundress. I packed up the rest of my things and made sure my costumes were hung up in the garment bag with my name on it. We didn't get to keep them. We left them in our dressing room to be picked up by one of the costume assistants after the show.

We had to stay backstage until all of the dances were done, but as soon as they were I headed for the lobby with Yumi and Amber and looked for my mom. She was relatively easy to find, since she was tall, like me. I spotted her carrying a giant bouquet of pink daisies.

"Mom, you didn't have to get me flowers," I said, even though lots of other parents had brought flowers for their kids. I saw Yumi's dad present her with a bouquet of white roses.

"You were so beautiful!" my mom said. "Let me take a picture!"

"Okay. That's enough," I finally said. How many pictures did she need of me standing in the lobby, holding my flowers?

"That first costume was beautiful!" she continued to gush. "You looked just like a real ballerina! And the second dance was amazing!"

"Thanks," I said. "I almost fell during my exit."

"I didn't notice. You looked perfect to me," she said, still smiling.

"Thanks, Mom," I said. I could have done the chicken dance in a monkey suit and my mom would still tell me it was the most beautiful thing she had ever seen. "Is it okay if I go say 'bye to my friends?"

"Of course! I'll meet you just outside," she said.

I found Yumi with her roses and Amber holding a bouquet of blue and purple orchids.

"Fancy," I said to both of them. My pink daisies seemed a bit childish next to theirs.

"I love daisies," Yumi said. "They're super pretty."

"Thanks," I said. "So—see you in two weeks?"

"Ah, the worst part of the year!" Amber groaned. "Fourteen days to kill between recital and summer session!"

I laughed and gave both of them a hug. It was going to be a long two weeks.

Three

The next morning I got up to find my mom had made pancakes with banana slices for breakfast—our favorite breakfast. My daisies were now in a glass vase in the center of the kitchen table. I dug into my pancakes, but my mom just picked at hers.

"Is something wrong?" I asked.

"Natalie, there's something I have to tell you," my mom said.

"What is it?" I asked, my appetite suddenly gone.

"It's my job." Mom works as an environmental geologist. "I've accepted a new project, but it means I'll be working up north for the entire summer."

"Oh," I said. "So I have to go with you? I take it they don't have ballet schools up there."

"Well, no..." my mom said. "I can't bring you with me. I would love to, but there would be nothing for you to do, and I'll be working long hours on the survey site..."

"So...if I'm staying here, how will I get to ballet class?"

"I know you're fifteen, but I don't think it's a good idea for you to be by yourself all summer," my mom said. "I already talked to your aunt and uncle in Windsor. They've agreed to have you stay with them."

"In *Windsor*? Why are you telling me this now? Why didn't you even ask me?" My voice was shaky, like it gets right before I start crying.

"This job is important to my career," my mom said. "And it's good money, which will make it easier to afford your dance classes. I waited until now to tell you so it wouldn't ruin your last week of school and your dance recital."

My face burned. I knew she was right about ballet class being expensive. And everything else that went with it—ballet slippers, pointe shoes, leotards, tights, stage makeup...

"Why can't I go stay with Dad for the summer?" I asked. When I was eleven, I visited him for two weeks when he was living in Germany. I haven't seen him since.

"It's too expensive to send you to China," my mom said. "And your dad is so busy and just... well, he wouldn't know what to do with you for an entire summer."

"But...I haven't even seen Aunt Lydia and Uncle Nolan since I was a little kid. I don't even remember what they look like."

"You'll have fun with your cousins," my mom said, still trying hard to sell the idea.

"They're just a bunch of strangers to me."

"Your dad's brother and his wife are the closest family we have, honey."

"Why can't I stay with Amber or Yumi?" I asked.

"I feel more comfortable leaving you with family," my mom said. "Before Lydia and Nolan moved to Windsor, your father and I were really close with them. I shouldn't have lost touch with them after your dad left. I think it's time for you to get to know your cousins again."

"Will I at least be able to find some ballet classes there?" I asked.

My mom sighed. "I feel like we're already imposing on them enough. I don't want to ask them to drive you back and forth to ballet classes. Your aunt and uncle both work and already have three other kids to take care of—"

"So you're sending me away to some other city to live with people I don't even know *and* I can't dance for the entire summer?"

"I'm afraid so," my mom said. "But it's only two months. It'll go by quick. Summers usually do."

"This isn't fair at all," I told her, but I knew it had already been decided. Mom wouldn't be doing this if there was another option.

"I'm sorry," my mom said. "I'll miss you. And we'll talk on the phone and email."

I nodded. There were no words left for how angry and upset I was.

"When do I have to leave?" I finally asked.

"This Thursday. So you still have a little time with your friends and time to pack, okay?"

I had to swallow the lump in my throat. I didn't trust my voice, so I just nodded again. I went to my room, leaving my plate of pancakes behind. I threw myself on my bed. I could hear my mom cleaning up the breakfast dishes.

I looked at the ballet posters on my blue-painted walls: one of Misty Copeland of American Ballet Theater and another of iconic Canadian dancer Karen Kain doing an arabesque penché. This wasn't just going to be a summer away from home and my friends. It'd be a summer away from *ballet*. But my mom was right—my aunt and uncle were letting me stay at their house, so I couldn't ask them to drive me to ballet classes too.

I sighed and rolled over to grab my phone.

"Hello?" Yumi answered.

"Hi. It's Natalie," I said. "I have some bad news."

"*What*?" Yumi asked.

"I'm not going to be able to do the summer session with you and Amber," I told her.

"Oh! Natalie!" Yumi said with a gasp. "Why not?"

I explained.

"That really sucks. We have to have a slumber party before you leave!" Yumi said. "Did you tell Amber yet?"

"No, I'm going to call her right now." We said our goodbyes.

After I'd told Amber, we made plans to have our slumber party at my place the night before I had to leave.

Amber and Yumi came over on Wednesday night. We laid out our sleeping bags and pillows in a row on the living room floor, nestled between the couch and the TV. My mom had promised to leave us alone for the night while she did some packing. Amber had brought a copy of our recital that her dad had recorded.

"Are you packing any dance stuff?" Yumi asked as one of the senior classes opened the show.

"Yes," I said. "I packed my tights and leotards, my ballet slippers and pointe shoes. I'm hoping I'll be able to find somewhere at their house to practice by myself. I don't want to fall behind."

"I don't think you'll fall behind," Yumi said. "You're the best dancer in our class!"

"I am most definitely *not*!" I said and hit Yumi with my pillow. "*You* are!"

"Hey!" she said, smacking me with her pillow.

"You guys! I'm trying to watch the recital!" Amber said, hitting both of us with her pillow.

I hit Amber back, and she fell onto Yumi in a fit of giggles. Her laughing was contagious, and Yumi and I began to giggle too. Finally we calmed down enough to watch our own class on the TV. We saw ourselves gracefully dance on stage in our purple "Waltz of the Flowers" costumes. I sighed. The only thing I was going to miss more than my two best friends was dancing.

Four

The drive to Windsor, about five hours south of Toronto, was boring—nothing but flat fields, some trees and giant wind turbines. Finally we turned off the highway and drove until we reached my cousins' neighborhood, which was row upon row of the exact same house in various shades of brown and gray.

"This is it," my mom said as she pulled up to a brown brick house.

I carried my suitcase up to the front door, but before we even knocked, the door swung open.

"Helen!" my uncle said as he hugged my mom tightly. "It's been so long! It's great to see you again. And Natalie! Look how tall you are! I hope you remember me."

I nodded, even though he only seemed vaguely familiar. I took a step back. He got the message and didn't try to hug me.

"It's good to see you, Nolan," my mom said with a smile. We followed my uncle inside.

A brunette woman and three girls were waiting in the hallway.

"So!" my Uncle Nolan said as he clasped his hands together. "They're here!" My aunt Lydia, I'm guessing, smiled and gave me a quick hug.

"And these are your cousins," Uncle Nolan said. "You've all met before, but it was a long, long time ago." My mom and my aunt both looked a bit embarrassed.

"Fiona," said one of the girls, formally extending a hand for me to shake. She had long brown hair like her mom and freckles on her nose.

"Lissa," the second girl said. She looked just like Fiona but was not quite as tall. Twins but not identical, I thought.

"They're both fifteen, like you," said Uncle Nolan.

"And I'm Molly," my smallest cousin said. She had auburn hair and freckles all over. "I'm twelve."

"You'll be sleeping in Molly's room," Aunt Lydia said. "There's more room in there, since the twins already share a room. Why don't you show her where it is, Molly?"

Great, I thought. I have to share with the youngest one.

I followed Molly upstairs. Along the way she informed me that she had bunk beds and she was willing to give me the top bunk and that her goldfish's name was Henry. She talked a mile a minute.

Her room was painted pale green and had a big window looking out into their backyard. I could see a large back lawn and a flower garden. Next to Molly's dresser was a rectangular fish tank on a stand. The fish swimming around the fake plants and sunken pirate ship was bright orange with fancy fins.

"I thought goldfish lived in bowls," I said as I put my suitcase down.

"No. Absolutely not," Molly said very seriously. "Goldfish should *never* be kept in bowls. They produce too much waste and grow too large. They need at least twenty gallons of water and a proper filtration system. They're cold-water fish, so technically they don't need a heater, but it's good to have one, just to make sure the water's temperature stays stable."

"Oh...okay," I said, pretending as best I could that all the information she was downloading on me was fascinating.

"C'mon, I'll show you the rest of the house," Molly said, and I followed her back downstairs.

I was surprised to see my mom standing at the door. It looked like she was ready to leave already.

"Sorry, honey, I really have to get going," my mom said as she drew me into a big hug. "It's just two months. It will fly by. I love you. I'm going to miss you *so* much."

"I love you too," I said quietly.

My mom waved one last time before driving away. For the first summer ever, I couldn't wait for September.

Five

"Your mom told us you like to dance," Aunt Lydia said at dinner that night.

"Would you like to go to the girls' dance class tonight?" Uncle Nolan asked.

My cousins did ballet? Maybe this summer wouldn't be so bad after all!

"I'd love to," I said almost immediately.

After dinner I unpacked my tights and leotards and changed into them. I covered up with a pair of lightweight track pants and a T-shirt. I tucked my pink ballet slippers and pointe shoes into my dance bag along with the bottle of water my aunt had given me and hopped into the minivan with my cousins. Aunt Lydia drove us to the local community center.

It looked nothing like ballet class back home. In the hallway warming up was a dozen or so kids, ranging from ten years old into their late teens. I spotted a couple of boys in the group. Most of the dancers wore shorts and T-shirts. My cousins tried to introduce me to a few people, but there were so many names and faces I was having trouble remembering them all.

The classroom door opened and a young woman let a group of little students out. The older kids filed into the classroom. I saw some kicking off their street shoes and rummaging in their dance bags, so I took off my track pants and slipped on my ballet slippers.

"Um…" said my cousin Fiona. "You can leave your pants on."

"What?" I asked and looked up to see that everyone else was still wearing shorts and T-shirts and lacing up black shoes over their socks. No one was wearing tights and leotards. No one was wearing pink ballet slippers.

I could feel my face growing hot. I wasn't sure what type of dance class this was, but it definitely wasn't ballet. I had just assumed when Aunt Lydia said *dance* that it must be ballet. They all stared at me. I grabbed my bag and ran from the room.

"Natalie! Wait!" Molly called after me.

I found the sign pointing to the bathroom and kept running. I found the first empty stall and slammed the door shut behind me. I quickly put my street clothes back on.

"Natalie?" Molly said, entering the bathroom.

I didn't answer. I felt incredibly stupid. And embarrassed. And a little bit pissed at my cousins for not telling me we weren't going to a ballet class.

"Natalie? I can see your feet. I know you're in here," Molly said.

I heard the bathroom door open again.

"Is she okay?" It was my cousin Lissa.

"Come out, Natalie." And now Fiona. "We thought you knew we didn't do ballet. We're sorry."

I still didn't feel like answering.

"We're all going to go back in with you," Fiona said.

"Yeah, we'll just explain you didn't know. It will be fine," Molly said.

"We're really sorry," Lissa added.

They sounded sincere. I felt a little bit stupid for locking myself in a bathroom stall. Slowly I opened the door. I looked at all three of them, their faces concerned. I believed them. They hadn't tried to trick me.

"So, what kind of dance class is it?" I asked, trying to act like everything was cool.

"It's Irish dancing," Lissa said. "It's really fun."

"You'll probably pick it up quickly, since you dance already," Molly said.

"Yeah, we heard your mom say you're really good at ballet," Fiona added.

"I guess I can try it out," I said. Better than hiding out in the bathroom until my aunt picked us up.

As we walked back down the hall I could hear upbeat music flowing from the dance classroom. It sounded like a fiddle. When I stepped back in the room with my cousins, the dancers had formed two straight lines in front of the one wall that had mirrors on it. They were jumping from one foot to the other and pointing the opposite foot. Their arms were held straight down at their sides.

"Cuts!" the teacher called and then noticed I had returned with my cousins.

The dance students continued to jump from one foot to the other, this time bringing up the opposite leg, as the teacher made her way over to us.

"Come join the warm-up, girls," the teacher said to my cousins. She walked over to me with her arm extended and a big smile on her face. "My name is Anna. Are you Natalie?"

"Yes," I said, shaking her hand.

"I understand you're a cousin of the Quinn girls?"

I nodded.

"Their mom called ahead. She told me you'd be coming today and that you did ballet. You can wear your ballet slippers if you like—they're pretty similar to the ones we wear for this class," Anna said.

I looked at the black shoes all the students were wearing. Soft leather, like my ballet slippers, but with crisscross laces up the whole top of the foot and a flat brown bottom.

"Try following along with the warm-ups," Anna said. "And then I can have one of the students teach you sevens."

"Okay, thanks," I said.

"Points again, class!" Anna called and guided me toward the back line of dancers. One of the boys gave me an encouraging smile. He had floppy brown hair that bounced around every time he jumped.

I smiled back as I began to try the point and jump. I was just getting the hang of it when Anna called for the class to switch it up again. "Point hop backs!"

I had to stop a moment to watch the others. I realized they were doing the same step as before but adding an extra hop. I gave it a try and realized it wasn't quite as hard as it looked.

"Good, Natalie!" Anna said.

I was pleased she had noticed, but right after that I lost my balance. I felt my face grow warm as the boy next to me glanced over.

"Cuts!" Anna called.

The students began to kick one bent leg up while jumping from one foot to the other. It kind of reminded me of watching the soccer team warm up at school—except they, of course, were kicking balls, not dancing.

"Good job!" Anna said as she turned off

the music. "Thomas, will you take Natalie out and teach her sevens? Everyone else, pair up for your reels!"

The boy with the floppy hair smiled at me again. He seemed like he was around the same age as me or maybe a year older.

"I'm Thomas," he said. "C'mon, I'll teach you your first reel step."

I followed him out into the hall.

"Okay. Newbie basics!" Thomas said. "The first thing you do before starting any dance is stand in first position."

I watched as he arranged his feet into a familiar position—his left toe was pointed to the left side and his right toe was pointed to the right, with his right heel touching his left toe. I put my feet in what I knew as ballet fifth.

"Great turn out!" he said.

I smiled and shrugged. Who knew Irish dancers turned their feet out just like ballet dancers?

"And then you point," Thomas said, stretching out his right foot into a perfect ballet tendu. I did the same.

"Here," Thomas said, bending down and nudging my foot over a bit so it would be crossed over my left foot. "Always make sure you keep your legs crossed."

I felt awkward. Apparently it *wasn't* exactly the same as a ballet tendu.

"Then you rise," Thomas said, bringing his feet together and standing on his tiptoes, which I knew as relevé in fifth in ballet class. I rose onto my toes and he nodded. "Good. Now we cut, like we just did in warm-up."

I watched as he jumped and "cut" his right leg up over his left and then put it back down. He took a few little steps to the right.

"You try," he said.

I tried to do what he had shown me.

"Wait! I forgot something!" Thomas said, grabbing my arms, which had naturally gone into the position that felt most comfortable to me—a low ballet fifth, rounded and down in front of me.

"Arms down and at the sides," Thomas said as he placed my arms.

Right. I'd seen that in the class. I felt a bit awkward as he held my arms down straight along my body. I had never had a male dance teacher before, and definitely not one as young (and cute) as Thomas. I was trying hard not to think about this as Thomas showed me the steps. It would only make me more nervous.

"Go ahead—try again with arms tucked in now," Thomas said.

Holding my arms straight felt a bit funny— like half of my body wasn't even dancing. I began again. I stood in "first," pointed and rose up on my tiptoes. Then I cut my right leg and tiptoed to the right. It felt a little bit like a pas de bourrée.

"Excellent!" Thomas said with a grin.

Thomas continued to teach me the rest of the "step"—it was actually a series of steps involving cuts, bourrées and hop backs. More like learning a whole combination. Then Thomas told me I had to reverse it! I started over, learning the same step on my left side.

"Now to music," he said, pointing to the classroom door where we could hear Celtic music playing.

Tapping into the beat of the music, we did the whole step together, both right and left.

"You're a natural," Thomas said. "Let's go back in so Anna can see."

While I was pretty proud of how quickly I'd picked it up, my stomach flipped over at the thought of having to dance in front of the whole class.

Six

I followed Thomas into the classroom, where Anna gave us a nod and a smile. Thomas led me to the back of the line of the pairs preparing to dance. I watched as my cousin Fiona and another girl both stood ready in Irish first position. They pointed and rose to their tiptoes before beginning to dance. Suddenly, their feet were a flurry of points, cuts, kicks and hops. They flew across the studio, keeping their arms and upper bodies perfectly straight. The girls in front of us took their turn next. Then it was time for Thomas and me.

"I'm going to go out there and start with you. You show them what you've learned, and then I'll do my own steps," he said.

He waited in first position with me, and I followed as he pointed his right foot and then rose onto his toes. He nodded to me right before we were to begin the first cut and move to the right. I felt my heart quicken as I realized the whole class was watching us. I made it through the entire sequence he'd taught me—I was a little shaky and didn't feel very graceful, but at least I kept in time with the music. Everyone clapped. Molly pulled me over to the wall, where the rest of the class was standing, while Thomas did his own steps. He moved across the entire room with intricate footwork and jumps. I noticed his shoes were different than the slippers the girls wore. The black leather shoes laced up like a regular running shoe and had small wooden heels. Thomas even managed to click his heels a few times during his dance.

The class moved on to what Anna called light jigs. Anna asked me to observe and promised I would learn one soon. Then they did slip jigs. The music was a bit slower and very pretty. I watched as my cousins moved gracefully and with confidence. The slip jig was beautiful.

Then students were given a break to grab a drink and change into their hard shoes. These kind of looked like tap shoes, black with a heel and a tap part under the front of the foot and under the heel. They laced up like a regular shoe, and some of them had decorative buckles on top.

The rest of the class was much noisier as all the students warmed up. Anna suggested I go over my sevens, but I couldn't help watching. Two by two they went through their hard-shoe steps to music. I was amazed at how fast they could move their feet and by how many different sounds they could make!

After everyone had done at least two different hard-shoe dances, the class ended. Molly came over to where I was practicing.

"We all bow to our teacher at the end of class," she whispered.

"Hey, just like ballet," I told her.

Instead of the grande reverence we did at the end of ballet class, the Irish-dance students simply pointed their right feet out as if they were going to begin dancing, but instead of going into relevé they bowed at their waists, still keeping their arms along their sides. I followed suit, and Molly gave me a nod to let me know I had done it right. I wanted to make sure I was properly thanking Anna for the wonderful class.

* * *

"So, how did it go?" Aunt Lydia asked as I hopped into the minivan with my cousins after class.

"Natalie's great. She already knows how to do sevens!" Molly said.

"Would you want to continue to go to dance class with the girls?" Aunt Lydia asked. "I know it's not ballet, but if you like it, I'll sign you up for the summer."

I looked at my cousins. All three of them were grinning.

"Yeah, it'll be fun!" Lissa said. "You already did so well in just one class."

"I don't know...I've only ever done ballet," I said.

"Maybe you could practice ballet at home," Fiona suggested.

"Shh! Don't tell her!" Molly said excitedly. "It'll be a surprise!"

"What? What will be a surprise?" I asked.

I saw Aunt Lydia glance back at us in the rearview mirror and smile.

Seven

"We should blindfold her!" Molly suggested.

"No, silly—we have to go down the stairs, and she might fall," Fiona said.

"What's downstairs?" I asked.

"The surprise!" Lissa said.

I followed the girls down to the basement. Fiona flicked on the lights and I found myself standing in...*a dance studio*! The entire basement had hardwood floors, perfect for dancing on, and there were tall rectangular mirrors hanging side by side, covering an entire wall.

"You have your own home dance studio?" I asked in astonishment.

"Pretty neat, right?" Fiona said. She began to skip around.

"We even have music," Lissa said as she walked over to the entertainment cabinet.

She opened it up and then connected her phone to the stereo inside. She scrolled through until she found a song she liked—a popular song I had heard on the radio, though I couldn't remember what it was called.

Lissa began dancing around the room—but more in a style you might see in a music video, *not* Irish dancing. Her sisters joined in, but then they joined hands and made a circle. They started doing cuts and sevens together, finding the beat in the song to coincide with their Irish-dance steps.

"C'mon!" Molly said and motioned for me to join in the circle.

I shook my head no.

"*C'mon!*" said Fiona and Lissa together.

Reluctantly I joined the circle between the twins. I felt silly trying to keep up with their quick feet. Fiona then let go of my hand and grabbed Molly's. Lissa grabbed both of my hands. We spun around the room with our partners.

"I'm too dizzy!" Lissa said and let herself fall to the floor, pulling me down with her.

Fiona and Molly collapsed next to us.

"Okay, girls! That's enough—time to shower and off to bed!" Aunt Lydia called down the stairs.

"Party pooper," said Molly and stuck out her tongue.

Lissa turned off the music and yawned.

"We *are* helping at the store tomorrow," Fiona said. "Dad wants us there bright and early, unfortunately."

"The store?" I asked.

"Our dad owns an aquarium store," Molly explained.

"And he forces us to help him once a week over the summer—on delivery day," Lissa said, sounding annoyed.

That's why Molly knows so much about goldfish, I thought as we headed upstairs.

As I lay in bed I sent a quick text to Yumi and Amber.

So it turns out my cousins are Irish dancers. Should I take class with them? It's basically that or nothing at all. But—they have their OWN dance studio. I can practice ballet in their house!

Yumi texted back right away:

Sounds cool. Some sort of dancing would be better than nothing, right? You'll still be in shape come September. BTW—super cool about the home studio! I wish.

* * *

The next morning we all woke up early so the girls could help their dad in his store—Quinn's Aquariums. I went along too.

"I hate helping at the store," Fiona whispered to me on the drive over. "It's *so* boring."

"No it's not," Molly said. "Did you know that there are twenty-five thousand identified species of fish on Earth? It's estimated that there may still be over fifteen thousand fish species that haven't even been discovered!"

"No, I didn't," I told her. I wasn't really listening. I glanced down at my phone. Still nothing from Amber. I had stayed up late texting with Yumi—apparently, Madame Lebrun was teaching this year's summer session and was refusing to do any of the fun stuff Michelle usually did.

"She probably doesn't care," said Lissa.

"Hey! Don't listen to those grumps!" Uncle Nolan called from the driver's seat. "And you never know. Maybe Natalie will turn out to like fish as much as Molly and I do!"

"I love fish," Molly said, grinning. "And shrimp. And snails. They're so cute!"

"Snails are *not* cute," Fiona said, looking disgusted.

"Oh, I love snails so much!" Molly said. "They've got little antennas and little round mouths...Just you wait, Natalie. You'll see how cute they are!"

Lissa and Fiona both rolled their eyes. I wasn't sure who I was going to agree with—I didn't know that much about fish and other underwater creatures. I'd never really paid much attention to them—maybe they were cute and I'd just never noticed? I slipped my phone into my pocket. I would try Amber again later.

Uncle Nolan's store was in a small plaza that also had a diner, a shoe store and a dollar store. Quinn's Aquariums was the farthest on the left and had a bright blue sign with the store name in yellow and different-colored fish swimming around the words.

Uncle Nolan let us in and the girls walked around, helping switch on the main lights and all the lights for the various aquariums. A bubbling, flowing sound filled the store. It smelled a bit... fishy. I guess that should have been expected.

I followed Molly as she switched on the lights and said her hellos and good mornings to all the aquatic creatures.

"Here's the golden apple snails," she said, pointing to an aquarium full of pink snails with bright yellow shells. "Watch this," she said. She reached under the aquarium's cabinet and pulled out a container of pellets. She dropped in a few brown pellets, which sank to the gravel. The snails all began to make their way toward the bottom of the tank, their antennae moving every which way, searching for the breakfast they'd detected going past.

"Cute, right?" Molly said expectantly.

They were pretty fun to watch, but they still seemed a bit icky—I felt they belonged in the same category as bugs and spiders. I was happy they were contained in the glass aquarium.

"*So not cute*," Fiona said in a singsong voice as she walked by with another container of fish food. She sprinkled some in other aquariums nearby and then scowled. "Uck. Fish food *stinks*."

"How are we doing, girls? Everyone getting their breakfast?" Uncle Nolan asked as he took out a blue net and a bucket.

"Dad's going to do the dead scoop," Molly said. "That's the more...*not fun* job."

"Dead scoop?" I asked.

"Yeah, we have to make sure there are no dead fish floating in the tanks when we open for customers," Molly explained.

"Ew," I said.

"*Exactly!*" Lissa said. "Fish are *gross*, not cute."

"Just wait until she sees the kissing gouramis!" Molly said and grabbed my arm to drag me over to a big display tank at the front of the store.

Inside the tank there was an abundance of pale pink fish—all making kissy faces. Sometimes they'd even go up to other fish and lock lips, like they were actually kissing!

"Okay, these are kind of cute," I said with a laugh.

"Ha!" Molly said to her sisters. "I knew these ones would win her over!"

* * *

The girls spent the rest of the day helping their dad in the store. The weekly shipment of merchandise arrived, and I helped unpack the boxes. Customers began to arrive. Fiona and Lissa mostly stuck with sweeping and stocking the shelves with fish food and aquarium decorations while Molly helped her dad talk to customers about fish and scooped their purchases into clear plastic bags to take home. Susan, the only actual employee at the store, worked the cash register.

"Do you want to try catch some minnows for Mr. Stevenson?" Molly asked me, nodding toward an elderly man.

I shrugged. "Okay."

"Any five will do. My turtle isn't picky about what his lunch looks like," said Mr. Stevenson.

I took the net from Molly and dunked it in the water. The little fish immediately swam away from the net. I kept trying to sneak up on them from behind, but I wasn't fast enough. I eventually caught two and deposited them into a bag full of water, but I could tell by Mr. Stevenson's fidgeting that I was taking too long.

"Um, why don't you catch the rest?" I said, handing the net back to Molly.

"Sure," Molly said. She easily scooped up three more minnows.

"Thank you," Mr. Stevenson said.

"You're very welcome!" said Molly.

By five o'clock the store was closed for the day, and it was time for us to head home. I checked my phone on the drive back. Still no messages from Amber.

Eight

On Saturday there was another Irish-dance class to go to. My cousins went to dance class Tuesdays, Thursdays and Saturdays—*all year long*!

I joined in the warm-ups and did the reel steps Thomas had taught me at the last class, but once again I didn't move on to light jig and slip jig with the rest of the class. Anna didn't want to overwhelm me, and Irish dance was a lot different than ballet. I continued to practice my reel steps. Everyone worked on their own steps at their own skill level even though they danced together.

"Everyone helps each other out," Thomas explained as Anna asked Fiona to show a younger girl her slip jig step. "When Anna sees a dancer is ready to move on and try a harder set of steps, she'll ask one of the more advanced dancers to show them."

The students changed their shoes and began to run through their hard-shoe dances, which were called treble jigs and hornpipes. There were a few kids who didn't have hard shoes yet. I was happy I wasn't the only one going over the steps in soft shoes.

"Okay, so who is going to the *feis* next weekend?" Anna asked at the end of class.

Almost the whole class raised their hands, including my cousins and Thomas. I noticed Molly's hand was only halfway up.

"Wonderful! I'll see you there!" Anna said. "You're all going to be amazing!"

Anna bowed to her class, and I bowed back with the rest of the students.

"What's a...what did Anna call it? It sounded like...fish...or flesh," I asked Molly as we walked out of class.

"A feis," Molly said, pronouncing the word as *fesh*. "It's an Irish-dance competition. Ugh."

"You don't like them?" I asked her.

"I never win *anything*," Molly said. "I hate going. I'd rather be at the store helping Dad.

I'd rather scoop the dead floaters than go to a feis!"

*   *   *

That night I was able to chat on the phone with my mom.

"You're dancing with your cousins? That sounds wonderful!" my mom said.

"Well, it's not the same. You know, as ballet. I'm going to be behind when I get back."

"But you're having fun with your cousins. I really wish you got to see them more often."

"Yeah, they're okay. Molly is pretty cute, I guess. She's really into fish."

"Mm-hmm. That sounds wonderful!" my mom said. She sounded distracted.

"And...Uncle Nolan turned into a fish. And Aunt Lydia was totally okay with it," I said.

"Oh yes, that sounds like fun," she said.

"Mom."

"Yes?"

"Are you even listening?"

"Yes, of course I am," she said.

"So you're not worried about Uncle Nolan turning into a fish?"

"Oh," my mom said. "Look, Natalie, maybe now's not a good time. I'll call you tomorrow, okay?"

"Yeah, okay. Good night, Mom," I said.

"Good night, Natalie. I love you."

"I love you too," I said, but she had already hung up.

Nine

The morning of the feis my cousins woke up at the break of dawn. Or maybe even before—I swear, the sun wasn't even up yet! They were all rushing around the house, their hair in curlers, making sure they had everything they needed for the day's events.

"Where are my socks?" Fiona asked me.

"Um...on your feet?" I said. She was already wearing a pair of purple socks.

"No, not *these* socks! My *dance* socks!" she said. "Oh, never mind! You won't know where they are!" She rushed back down the hall to her room.

"Girls? Are you almost ready?" Aunt Lydia called from the front door. "We were supposed to leave ten minutes ago!"

"I'm ready," Molly said glumly and came out of her room carrying a green duffel bag and a garment bag.

Fiona and Lissa followed close behind her, both with backpacks and garment bags. They all had colorful curlers in their hair.

"But...your hair?" I asked as I followed them out to the minivan. "You're...leaving the house like that?"

"Yeah, we take them out when we get there," Fiona said. "For maximum curliness."

"It's so embarrassing," Molly groaned. "We don't even have tinted windows in the van."

"Oh, shush, Molly. You can take them out during the drive over if you want," Aunt Lydia said.

The feis was about two hours away. During the car ride I helped Molly take the purple foam curlers out of her hair.

"We wouldn't have to wear them if we had wigs," Lissa said.

"Wigs?" I asked.

"Yeah, most of the girls you'll see today will be wearing curly wigs so they don't have to worry about doing their hair. They just pop on their wigs. It's *so* much easier," Fiona said.

"Mom says they're too expensive," Lissa said with a frown.

"They *are* too expensive!" Aunt Lydia said. Clearly they had had this argument before. "Especially when I have to buy *three* of them!"

"I don't need a wig," Molly said. "I could just, you know, not go."

"Don't be ridiculous," Aunt Lydia said. "I think you girls look beautiful with your own hair and not those silly wigs."

When we arrived at the high school where the competition was being held, I noticed several girls with curly hair. Lissa and Fiona were happy to point out the wigs. I felt a little out of place with my hair pulled up in a ponytail. I waited with my cousins and Aunt Lydia in the registration line. All three got numbers to pin to the front of their dance dresses. Little wooden stages a couple of inches high had been set up around the large gymnasium. We had to walk around to find out which stages the girls would be dancing on and at approximately what time. The first dance of the day for the twins was the two-hand reel.

Lissa helped Fiona with her curlers as Aunt Lydia helped Lissa with hers. The twins then changed into their matching school dresses—white with navy-blue Celtic knots. The dresses were long-sleeved and knee-length. The girls pulled their white dance socks as high as they would go.

There was an accordionist on the corner of every stage to play for the dancers. I stood with Aunt Lydia and Molly by the stage where the twins were going to be dancing the two-hand reel. There were five other sets of partners hanging out there too. I recognized Thomas and a girl named Shaina from class.

I was mesmerized as the musician began to play and the dancers performed on the tiny stage. Fiona and Lissa danced beautifully, as did Thomas and Shaina. I clapped for them as they bowed at the end of their performance, first to the judge sitting at a table in front of the stage and then to the musician.

"So, who won?" I asked as they all left the stage area and new dancers began to line up.

"We have to wait and see. We check over there if they have our numbers," Fiona said, pointing to a long row of boards, still mostly empty, and a long table full of boxes of medals. Volunteers stood at the tables, ready to post results and hand out the medals.

"Oh, they're doing the Tir na Nog!" Lissa said, looking over at a stage with a bunch of little kids.

"Let's go watch!" said Fiona.

Molly and I followed the twins over.

"What is this?" I asked.

"Tir na Nog," Molly said. "The wee kids get to dance. It's just for fun. They usually give them all a teddy bear and a medal when they're done."

Most of the boys and girls wore dressy clothes, but not traditional Irish dress like the older competitors. One at a time they skipped around the stage and did a few little steps. They were adorable.

Molly's reel was next. She had already changed into her solo dress, which was much fancier than the "school dresses" her sisters had worn for their two-hand reel. Molly's dress was mint green with pink roses and silver sequins. She got onstage and was dancing beautifully until she froze and seemed to forget her steps for a moment. Her face turned crimson, but she started dancing again. When she was done, she quickly bowed to the judge and the musician and went back to her spot in line.

"Ah, she always does this at competitions!" Lissa said. "She forgets her steps!"

When we checked the boards later, we found out that the twins had come in third place for their two-hand reel. They registered with a feis volunteer, who happily gave them their bronze medals. Molly did not place in her solo reel.

The rest of the day passed in a blur—the girls going from stage to stage, dancing and then checking in at the results board. Fiona and Lissa both had fancy solo dresses like Molly's. Fiona's was pure white and covered in colorful sequins and gems, while Lissa's was purple with turquoise curlicues and silver sequins. They both wore sparkly rhinestone headbands.

Fiona ended up with a silver medal for her slip jig, and Lissa got two more bronze medals— one for her reel and one for her hornpipe. Molly didn't win any.

"Maybe next time," Aunt Lydia told Molly as they packed up their things to head home. Molly rolled her eyes, but I didn't think her mom noticed.

Watching the girls dance all day had made me itch to dance—but not Irish dancing. I was eager to practice ballet, to make sure I wasn't getting too rusty.

"When we get home, could I use the dance studio?" I asked on the drive back.

"It's all yours!" Molly said. "We're all danced out."

Ten

fter dinner I changed into my ballet tights and leotard. I slipped my leather ballet slippers on my feet and headed down to the dance studio. After their long day of dancing, my cousins were showering and resting.

I sent a quick text to Yumi before I got started.

Hey. Just went to my first Irish-dance competition with my cousins. Was pretty interesting. How is Madame Lebrun?

I also decided to try Amber, even though I hadn't heard from her since I got to Windsor.

Hey, Amber. How is your summer? How is ballet class? Miss you. Miss ballet.

I fooled around with the stereo until I found a radio station that played classical music. My phone beeped. It was from Amber:

Hey. Ballet is good. Madame No Fun is really working us. It'll be good come September. You Irish-dance now?

I texted back:

Just trying some classes with my cousins. I can't go to ballet here. Wish I could.

I got another text from Amber:

Hopefully we'll still be in the same class come September.

I reread the text. *Hmmm.* Sometimes students were moved up to more difficult classes if they were excelling, and sometimes they were moved down to an easier class if their original class was progressing faster than they were. Was Amber suggesting I might be moved to a less advanced class because I missed one summer of ballet?

Whatever. I slid my phone across the hardwood floor and into the wall. I did my barre exercises in center floor, since there was no barre in this dance studio. Pliés, tendus and grande battements. It felt *so good* to be dancing ballet again. But with every move, Amber's text haunted me. Was I really falling behind? I carried on through my usual ballet-class routine, doing exercises in port de bras (carriage of the arms) and the faster, allegro movements, including sautés and pas de chat (fun jumps). Then I began to practice my pirouettes.

"Don't you get dizzy?" Molly was sitting at the bottom of the stairs.

I jumped mid-pirouette and nearly fell over.

"Oh! I'm sorry! I didn't mean to scare you," Molly said.

"It's okay, I just didn't know you were there," I said. "What did you say?"

"How do you spin and not get dizzy?" Molly asked.

"It's called spotting," I told her. "You pick a spot on the wall and keep your eyes on it until the very last moment—and then you snap your head around back to the same spot."

I demonstrated for her by marching in a circle and snapping my head around. Then I prepared in fourth position before demonstrating a double pirouette.

"That's amazing!" Molly said. "Ballet looks even harder than Irish dancing!"

"I don't know about that," I said, remembering all the intricate dance steps I'd seen at the feis that day. "Irish dancing is pretty challenging. And I've only learned a beginner reel so far."

"Irish dancing *is* challenging," Molly grumbled, pulling her knees up to her chest. "I hate going to competitions. I've never won a single medal— not ever! My sisters always place in at least one dance."

"Well, if you enjoy it, it shouldn't be about winning, right?" I said, wondering if I would still love ballet if I was moved to a different class. "You should just dance because you love to dance."

Molly was silent for a moment, staring at her toes. "But...I *don't* like dancing."

"Oh. I thought you did," I said, surprised. "You and your sisters seem to really enjoy yourselves! You go to class three times a week, you have your own dance studio—you're so lucky."

"I don't feel very lucky," Molly said. "I also don't really feel like dancing anymore."

"Oh," I said, walking over to sit next to her on the stairs. "Well, why don't you talk to your mom?"

"My mom loves that we all dance—she always wanted to dance when she was younger, but her parents could never afford classes. I don't want to disappoint her. Or my sisters," Molly said.

"I think they would understand," I said.

"No! You don't know them! Irish dance is *everything* to them! I can't tell them," Molly said and abruptly got up. She began to run up the stairs but stopped halfway to look back. "And you can't tell them either. Promise?"

"Okay," I said. "I promise."

I checked my phone. No new messages from Amber. No messages from Yumi. And none from my mom. I shut it off.

Eleven

At the next class Thomas showed me the second step for my reel—what would come after I did the sevens.

"Everyone has two steps—we do right and left of the first step, and then right and left of the second step," he explained. "That's what you'll do when you go to a feis."

"Oh, I don't know if I'll ever be going to a feis," I said. In ballet I had never competed—we only did dance examinations and the annual recital.

"There's one here at the end of August—you'll still be here, right?" he asked.

"Well, yes..." I said.

"Then why not make that your goal? Compete at the Rose City Feis!" Thomas said with a bright smile.

I found myself smiling back. His smiles were contagious. "We'll see," I said.

Thomas showed me what my second reel step would be—it was much more complicated than the first step.

"When do I get to learn a slip jig?" I asked.

Thomas laughed. "You're eager! Once you can show Anna you have your reel down, you can learn a light jig. Once you show her you can handle a reel *and* a light jig, she'll let you learn a slip jig. And then you can compete in all three at the feis!"

I nodded but didn't feel 100 percent committed to the idea. If I spent too much time Irish dancing, would my ballet dancing suffer?

* * *

I decided I was going to practice ballet in the basement studio for an entire day. I was tying up my pointe shoes when I got a text from Yumi telling me how hard the summer session was and how she had finally mastered her double pirouettes on pointe. I could do doubles in my leather ballet slippers, but definitely not on pointe. I wrote back congratulating her. Right after that Amber texted, asking if I had learned any new jigs.

I haven't learned any jigs yet. Only a reel.

I was just kidding.

Oh, right. Yumi says she can do double pirouettes on pointe now. That's pretty cool.

I guess. I mean, the whole class can now, thanks to Madame No Fun.

I just stared at the screen. The whole class could do doubles on pointe? Was she serious?

Wow. Congrats.

Well, gotta go. Have fun dancing like a leprechaun. Hope you still remember what a plié is in September.

I swallowed the lump that had formed in my throat. I was enjoying Irish-dance classes. Was that wrong? Amber made me feel like I was cheating on ballet. And she made me feel like I was only falling farther and farther behind. It didn't really matter how much I practiced ballet on my own—it wasn't the same as being in a real class. And it definitely wasn't the same as being in a ballet class with a teacher like Madame Lebrun.

I looked up at myself in the mirror and tucked a piece of flyaway hair behind my ear. I prepared in fourth and then tried to turn a double pirouette on pointe. I completely fell out of my turn. I tried again, this time only going for a single—but fell out of my turn again. I took a deep breath in and then let it out again. And tried again for a single. I couldn't stick my turn. I plunked myself down on the floor and tore off my shoes. What was the point?

I slipped on my leather ballet slippers and stood back up. If I was going to lose all my ballet technique over the summer anyway, why not practice the one dance form I was going to class for? I started going over my reel steps. I didn't care what Amber thought. Irish dancing wasn't a joke. It was hard. And a part of me was beginning to really love it.

Twelve

My cousins came down in the afternoon to practice their own steps and give me advice.

"Keep your legs crossed!" Fiona shouted at me.

"You can get up higher on those toes, ballerina!" Lissa called.

"Arms! Stop letting your arms flop around!" Molly said.

I finished what felt like my hundredth reel that day, pointed my foot and bowed to my cousins. I collapsed to the floor, exhausted. I could feel sweat trickling down my back.

"Dance like that during tomorrow's class and Anna will be sure to let you learn a light jig!" Fiona said.

"Really?" I asked, still lying on the floor, panting.

"Yeah. What's got into you anyway?" Lissa asked.

"I just—love watching the dancers do their slip jigs in class," I said, pushing myself to a sitting position. "I want to learn that dance. It's so graceful and beautiful! Thomas said if I do my reel well, I can learn a light jig next, and if I can do both my reel and light jig, I'll be allowed to learn a slip jig."

"I'm pretty sure you'll be learning a slip jig by the end of the summer," Molly said with a smile.

"Thomas also mentioned the Rose City Feis at the end of August. Would I be allowed to compete?" I asked, even though I wasn't completely sure about it yet.

"Yeah! Of course! We can ask Mom to register you," Lissa said.

"Why would you want to compete?" Molly asked.

"I don't know if I want to yet," I said. "But... Thomas mentioned it and..." I felt my cheeks growing hot. Darn it! I didn't want my stupid blush to give me away, but I could already tell my cousins were noticing. Lissa and Fiona exchanged a look and grinned at each other.

"You like Thomas!" Fiona declared.

"No!" I exclaimed, but my face got warmer.

"He is pretty cute," Lissa said with a shrug. "And you have been spending a lot of *one-on-one* time with him during class."

"He was teaching me my reel!" I said.

Fiona shrugged. "*All* the girls have a crush on Thomas."

"Do you?" I asked.

The twins exchanged a look again and then nodded.

"Like he'd ever notice us," Lissa said with a shrug. "It's just a silly crush. Shaina has her eye on him anyway—his two-hand-reel partner."

"Yeah, but Lissa *really* likes Riley," Fiona said.

This time is was Lissa's turn to blush.

"Who's Riley?" I asked.

"He's an Irish dancer from Guelph," Fiona explained. "Sometimes Lissa sees him at competitions."

"More like *stalks* him," Molly said.

"I do not!" Lissa shouted. "I've even talked to him! Once...two summers ago."

"Was he at the last feis we went to?" I asked.

"No," Lissa said with an exaggerated pout. "But maybe next feis..."

"*Maybe next feis*," Molly said teasingly.

"Shut up!" Lissa said and pushed Molly, who pretended to fall over.

"Boys are boring," Molly said. "Natalie, can you show Fiona and Lissa that ballerina spotting thing?"

"Um...okay," I said, happy that Molly had changed the subject. I didn't really want to talk about Thomas anymore. I wasn't sure how I felt about him. I mean, he was cute...and nice... but I was only going to be here for the summer. I shook my head and walked out to the center of the studio to turn some pirouettes. I wasn't on pointe now. I was determined to show my cousins what a perfect double looked like.

I did feel awkward at first—like I was showing off—but Fiona and Lissa seemed genuinely interested in learning about another dance form. After showing them the pirouettes (which I pulled off successfully) I taught them how to do pliés and tendus. I showed them the different positions of the feet. Molly sat at the bottom of the stairs, watching. She insisted she just wanted to watch and didn't want to try out the ballet steps.

"I think we'll stick with Irish dancing," Fiona said as she collapsed on the floor after trying out a series of fast-paced sautés.

I laughed and collapsed next to her. It felt wonderful to dance ballet again. But I was still excited about learning more Irish dancing.

Thirteen

Later that night I made my weekly call to my mom. She sounded tired and distracted—like she always did. I missed her and wished we could talk more—about Irish dancing, about ballet, about Amber. But it was like she couldn't really focus on what I was saying. I knew all her hard work was for us—to pay for our home, my ballet classes. I just wished I could see her and really talk to her.

During the next class I got a chance to show Anna my reel. She was impressed and asked a girl named Melodie to teach me a light jig. I was excited to learn the new dance, but a little disappointed that it wasn't Thomas teaching me.

The next day we were all at Quinn's Aquariums again, helping out Uncle Nolan. It was a quiet day with very few customers. I found myself practicing my new light jig between the rows of softly glowing aquariums. Uncle Nolan laughed when he saw me.

"So you have the Irish-dance bug too?" he said with a smile.

I shrugged. "I guess." But why did admitting that make me feel like I was cheating on ballet? What would Amber say?

"Why are you practicing so hard?" Molly asked. "It's not like it's very difficult for you. You're a natural, especially with your ballet background."

The door *ding*ed as a customer entered the store. Uncle Nolan went to help them.

"I really want to learn a slip jig by the end of the summer," I explained to Molly. "So I can compete in the Rose City Feis." *And to prove to Amber (and myself?) that this whole summer wasn't a waste of time.* "I mean, if I'm going to miss an entire summer of ballet, I might as well try to excel at the one kind of dance I *am* doing, right?"

Molly shrugged. "I could show you my stupid slip jig," she said.

"You could?" I asked, ignoring the word *stupid.*

"Sure," Molly said. "I'll teach you tomorrow. Then you can show Anna during our next class. Just don't tell my sisters. It'll be a surprise."

*   *   *

The following day Fiona and Lissa invited me to go bike riding with some of their friends, but I told them I'd rather stay home.

"Are you ready?" I asked Molly as soon as they'd left.

"Sure, let's go downstairs," Molly said.

We did a quick warm-up together.

"Okay then, with the slip jig, we start the same as all the other dances—in first position, point and rise," Molly said as she did the actions herself. I quickly did the same. "Then we're going to point your right foot twice and hop back, and then the same on the left..."

Molly patiently showed me the steps over and over. By dinnertime I was able to do them on my own. I practiced my reel and light jig too. And then I went back and did the new slip jig steps again, just to be certain I could do it on my own on Saturday. I wondered if Thomas would be impressed I had learned it so quickly.

I texted Yumi.

I learned a slip jig today. It's one of the more graceful dances.

Amber says you might not be in our class next year.

I hesitated before I replied.

I don't think I'm falling behind that much. I still practice ballet. And I'm still in shape from doing Irish dancing all summer. It's very fast-paced with lots of jumping.

It's not the same. Amber says Irish dancing is just a bunch of silly jigs, and you don't even use your arms.

I couldn't help but wonder what else Amber might be saying about me. And why? Yumi and Amber had been my two best friends for the past five years. I was having trouble understanding what I had done to Amber to suddenly make her so...*mean.* It wasn't my choice to leave for the entire summer. It wasn't my choice to fall behind in ballet. And so what if I was experimenting with another dance form? Why should she even be mad about that in the first place?

Irish dancing isn't silly. It's hard. My cousins have practiced for years to be able to place at competitions. There's even a world competition for Irish dancing.

Okay, okay. Amber says don't get your bloomers in a twist.

Amber was there? Reading Yumi's text messages with her? Whatever.

It's hard. Maybe you guys should try it before you knock it.

I waited for them to reply. Nothing. I shut my phone off. Maybe I wouldn't be returning to ballet.

Fourteen

On Saturday morning I could feel myself growing more and more nervous. My legs and arms felt shaky. But by the time we had finished our warm-ups in class, I was feeling more excited than nervous. We did our reels first, as usual, followed by our light jigs—and then it was time for the slip jigs. I went and got in line with the others, with Molly as my partner. Thomas gave me an odd look, but no one else seemed to notice. Fiona and Lissa were ahead of us. It wasn't until I had successfully completed my slip jig and walked off the dance space that I dared to look over at Anna. She gave me a puzzled look but kept silent. She did not smile. She did not congratulate me.

"What are you doing?" Thomas whispered as I sat on the floor. The rest of the class was now putting on their hard shoes. I noticed Fiona and Lissa frowning at me, but I had no idea why.

"I got Molly to teach me a slip jig—for the Rose City Feis," I told him.

"Did Anna know about that?" he asked.

"No, I wanted to surprise her," I said. I smiled, but he didn't smile back. Why was everyone acting so weird? I began to feel sick to my stomach. Had I danced horribly? It had felt all right.

When the dancers had done their treble jigs, hornpipes and set dances, we all rose for our final bow.

"Molly and Natalie—may I talk to you before you leave?" Anna said.

Fiona and Lissa said they'd wait outside. Molly and I walked over to Anna.

"Molly," Anna said, "did you teach Natalie your slip jig?"

"Yes," Molly answered, looking down.

"Did I ask you to do so?" Anna asked.

"No, miss," Molly said.

"I'm sorry," I jumped in. "I told her I was desperate to learn a slip jig, so she taught me hers." I could feel my palms growing sweaty.

"It's up to the teacher to decide when a student should learn a new step or dance. The teacher knows when her students are ready," Anna said. "Molly, you should know this. You've been dancing with me long enough. A student is never permitted to teach another student new steps outside of class."

"I'm sorry, miss," Molly said. "It's just that… she's already a ballerina and all…so I thought it would be okay."

"I understand that's why Natalie has been picking up the dance steps much quicker than the average beginner," Anna said, "but that's no excuse for ignoring the rules." She turned to me. "I understand that ballet classes are very strict and have rules too, just like we do. Isn't that correct, Natalie?"

"Yes," I said quietly. I thought of how hard I'd had to work before I was allowed to start classes on pointe. I would never have even bought pointe shoes before my teacher gave me permission. "I'm sorry."

"Apology accepted," Anna said. "You will not be doing that slip jig in class again until you've earned it. You may go now."

"We're very sorry," Molly said once more before grabbing my hand and pulling me out of the room.

"What was that about?" Aunt Lydia asked as we got to the minivan. I glanced at Fiona and Lissa, but their faces were blank. Clearly, they hadn't told their mother about my slip jig.

"Nothing," Molly said. "Anna just wanted to ask Natalie a few things about ballet classes, that's all."

As soon as we got home, Fiona and Lissa banged open the door of the room I shared with Molly.

"I suppose Anna set you straight?" Fiona said, glaring at Molly.

"Yes, I'm sorry! I already apologized!" Molly said, throwing herself onto her bed and burying her face in her pillows.

"You should apologize to Natalie too," Lissa said. "You knew better—Natalie didn't. But you taught her your steps anyway and got her in trouble. *And* you hid it from us!"

"I knew you wouldn't let me teach her!" Molly said. "And I knew how much Natalie wanted to learn a slip jig. But I didn't know everyone would be this angry!"

"But you know you're not supposed to teach steps outside of class!" Fiona said. "Natalie didn't. Apologize to Natalie."

"No, it's okay. Really," I said. I'd had no idea Molly was going to get into this much trouble. I felt awful.

"No, I want to apologize," Molly said, sitting up on her bed now, her face tear-stained. "I'm sorry, Natalie. I didn't mean to get you in trouble."

"It's okay."

The twins seemed satisfied.

"Don't do it again," Lissa said to both of us on their way out.

Fifteen

The next day Molly asked her dad if she could go with him to the aquarium shop. I figured she wanted to get away from her sisters.

"Can I come with you?" I asked.

She shrugged. "I guess so."

We stayed all day. It was a good distraction that kept me away from my phone. I hadn't received any more texts from Yumi or Amber, and I wasn't sure if I even wanted to. I managed to successfully bag a fish for a customer. It was a goldfish, which move a bit slower than the other ones.

"Good job!" Molly said.

"Thanks," I said. "You really like working here, don't you?"

Molly looked around at the aquariums with a sad smile. "Yeah, I do. I wish I could spend as much time here as I do at the stupid dance classes and competitions."

"Why don't you tell your parents that?" I asked. "I'm sure your dad would understand. I bet he would love to have you at the shop more."

Molly shrugged. "I already asked to quit dance, like, two years ago. My mom said no. She said I'd eventually get better and start winning medals. And then I would be happy she made me keep going. It hasn't happened yet."

"Maybe you should ask again," I said.

"It's no use!" Molly said.

Uncle Nolan came over to the aquariums.

"Everything okay, girls?" he asked.

"Yes," Molly said quickly and walked away.

"We're fine," I said and went to check on the new baby guppies.

*　*　*

The following weekend the girls were getting ready for another feis in a nearby town. Their hair was in curlers, they had packed up their school dresses and solo dresses in garment bags, and they were using roll-on sock glue to keep their white dancing socks in place.

"That does not look comfortable," I told them.

"It's not," Molly said.

"Is the glue really necessary?" I asked.

"Keeps your socks from falling down!" Lissa said cheerfully. The twins were always in a good mood on the way to a feis.

"'Cause your socks falling down is just the worst," Molly said, rolling her eyes.

I smiled. Irish dancing certainly had its quirks.

We arrived early and had more than enough time for the girls to register and get their numbers. The feis was set up in a large gymnasium on a college campus. The twins put on their matching school dresses so they would be ready for their two-hand reel. I was happy to see that Thomas would also be competing in the two-hand reel—but not so happy to see the beautiful Shaina at his side again.

The twins danced brilliantly, as usual. Thomas and Shaina also danced well. I made a point of walking over to Thomas as they left the stage and congratulating him on a job well done. Molly followed behind me.

"Thanks!" Thomas said.

"Yeah, thanks," Shaina said and then pulled Thomas off in the opposite direction.

"C'mon, Natalie, don't bother," Molly said.

"Don't bother what?" I asked.

"Flirting with Mr. Dancy-Pants," Molly said. "He's very obviously taken."

"Actually," Lissa said, as she followed my gaze toward Thomas and Shaina, "Thomas recently claimed he's *married* to dance."

"What does that even mean?" Molly asked.

"That he's dedicated to dance and has no time for silly girls," Fiona explained. "I think it makes sense. I've decided I want to be married to dance too, to keep focused so I can make it to the World Championships."

"*Pfft.* As if there are any boys interested in you," Molly said.

"Making it to Worlds would be amazing," Lissa said. "One day—we'll get there together," she finished, looking at her twin.

"Promise?" Fiona asked.

"Wouldn't want it any other way," Lissa said.

Molly began pretending to barf.

"Cut it out, Molly," said Lissa.

"If you train hard, Molly," Fiona quickly added, "you could make it too. All three Quinn sisters! At the World Championships together!"

"Yeah, that will never happen," Molly grumbled. "I mean, the part about me. You two go ahead. You can take over the world without me."

"I'd love to come watch that," I said. I tried to forget about Thomas. After all, I *was* leaving at the end of the summer.

Sixteen

I decided to wander around the vendor tables while my cousins went off to change into their solo dresses. All sorts of Irish-dance items were for sale, including the kind of white socks my cousins and other dancers wore and the black leather shoes. If I was going to be competing in the feis in August, I would need proper shoes, wouldn't I? My mom had given me some spending money for the summer. I was sure she would be okay with my using it to buy dance shoes. I stopped at one of the tables piled with shoes and socks.

"Thinking about buying your first pair of ghillies?" Thomas was suddenly standing right next to me. He was in his performance clothes—black dress pants and a blue dress shirt with a black vest and tie. I had to admit, he looked pretty handsome dressed up. I was used to seeing him in shorts and a T-shirt. Okay, that wasn't a bad look either.

"Pardon?" I said, stalling until I could string more words together.

"Ghillies," Thomas said, holding up a pair of the black leather dance shoes. "That's what these are called."

"Oh yeah," I said. "I mean...if I want to compete in the Rose City Feis and all...I thought I might..."

"You should definitely try out a feis this summer," Thomas said. "You'll win a medal for sure. You're a natural."

"Thanks," I said. I didn't want to know what shade of red I might be right now.

"Can I help you?" A woman on the other side of the table approached us. "Looking to buy some shoes?"

"Um...yes," I said. "And some socks."

"What size do you take?" the woman asked.

She dug out a pair and then motioned for me to sit on a nearby bench so I could try them on.

Thomas stayed by my side as the woman showed me how to tie them up properly.

"How do those feel?" she asked.

"Good," I said as I stood and pointed one foot in a tendu and then the other.

"Ghillies suit you," Thomas said. "Oh man. I better get going—my next dance is coming up soon."

"Okay. Um—break a leg!" I called after him.

"Thanks!" he called back and then got lost in the crowd of people.

"Shopping for new hard shoes too?" the vendor asked me.

"Oh no, just these are fine. I don't do hard shoe yet," I told her.

"Maybe next year," she said with a wink as she packed up my shoes and socks.

I paid her and then went off in search of my cousins and aunt, excited to show them my new purchases.

Aunt Lydia was where I had left her in the gymnasium, in a camping chair, reading a book. Molly was with her, looking uncomfortable and nervous.

"Look!" I said and opened the bag to show them my shoes and socks.

"Oh! Lovely!" Aunt Lydia said. "Now we *have* to sign you up for the Rose City Feis!"

"What did you buy?" Fiona asked as she and Lissa walked over in their solo dresses.

I showed them, and they clapped giddily.

"So exciting!" Lissa said. "I still have my first pair of ghillies!"

"C'mon, Molly, your reel will be starting soon," Aunt Lydia said, getting to her feet.

"Ours might be starting soon too," Fiona said. "We're going to go check our stage. See you later!"

I decided Molly needed my cheerleading more than the twins did, so I followed Aunt Lydia and her to the stage where Molly would be dancing. Molly checked in with the rest of the dancers her age and took a seat until the judge was ready. Aunt Lydia and I found a good spot in front to watch.

Molly and the other girls walked onto the stage single file, and then the accordionist began to play. Two by two the dancers did their reel steps— just like in class. Molly was in the second pairing.

She moved up with her partner, pointed her foot, rose up on her toes and began to dance. For all her grumbling and complaining, she was actually pretty good.

Molly was just about to start her second step when she lost her footing. She tumbled to the floor, landing hard on her side. The other dancer glanced in her direction but didn't miss a beat. Molly got back to her feet—but it was obvious she wasn't quite sure where to pick up. Her face was crimson.

"Oh no," I heard Aunt Lydia say softly.

Molly waited until she could begin her second reel step on her left, so she would finish around the same time as the other girl. It didn't look like she had injured herself. She bowed to the judge and the musician and then got back in line. She had to stand and wait until the rest of the girls were done, her face remaining a deep red.

"She's never fallen before," Aunt Lydia told me quietly. "I hope she's okay."

My stomach was in knots because of what I knew. Should I tell Aunt Lydia how Molly felt about dancing? That she didn't want to compete anymore? Or should I mind my own business and let Molly tell her mom when she was ready?

When the dancers finally finished and were allowed to leave the stage, Molly walked briskly away from the other girls. She hurriedly brushed past me and her mom and ran to the bathroom.

"Molly! Wait!" Aunt Lydia said, rushing after her.

I wasn't sure if I should follow. I decided I would, but I kept my distance. If it looked like this was strictly a mother-daughter situation, I'd be able to quietly back away. I followed Aunt Lydia into the ladies' washroom. I could see Molly's feet under the stall door. I could hear her sniffles.

"Molly? Honey? Are you okay? Did you hurt yourself?" Aunt Lydia asked.

"No!" Molly shouted. "Go away!"

They definitely needed some privacy. I headed back to our camp to find that the twins had already danced their reel and were eagerly awaiting their results.

"Where are Molly and Mom?" Lissa asked.

"Bathroom," I said, deciding to keep it short and simple.

"How did Molly do?" Fiona asked.

"She...um...well, she fell. But she wasn't hurt," I added quickly. "She got back up and finished her reel."

The twins exchanged worried looks.

"Is Molly upset?" Lissa asked.

"Um...yes," I said. "Your mom is with her though."

Fiona sighed. "I hope everything is okay."

"I'm sure she's fine," Lissa said. "C'mon. Let's go see how long we have until slip jig."

I went with them. Their slip jig was coming up soon. Some younger girls were onstage. I watched them dance—with grace but also with speed. They looked like butterflies gliding across the stage. I couldn't take my eyes off them. How much longer would I have to wait before I would be allowed to dance a slip jig?

Seventeen

On the way back to our camp, Lissa stopped dead in her tracks. She was looking over at the stage to her left. Fiona walked right into her.

"Oof!" Fiona said. "What are you doing? Learn how to walk."

"Stage three—sixteen and over," Lissa whispered to her sister, nodding toward one of the stages where a group of dancers waited. At least three of the dancers were boys.

"C'mon!" Lissa said, grabbing my arm and hurriedly walking over. "Thomas is in this group too." She winked at me.

"So?" I said, pretending not to care though I could feel my heart rate quicken.

As we got closer the twins slowed their steps and pretended to be casually walking by. We found a spot to watch as the competitors walked onstage. Thomas was in the first pairing. We watched as he performed his reel, making perfect clicks with the hard heels on his soft shoes.

As the next pair of boys got ready, Lissa grabbed Fiona's arm.

"Ouch!" Fiona said.

"It's Riley," Lissa whispered.

"I know!" Fiona said.

"*The* Riley?" I asked quietly.

"Yep. She's got it *bad*," Fiona said with a roll of her eyes.

"He watched my reel once. He told me I danced beautifully," Lissa said. "And he's so cute!"

Fiona rolled her eyes again but then turned her attention to Riley. He was wearing a green dress shirt and black dress pants. He did dance wonderfully—but I still thought Thomas was better. And cuter.

As the dance ended Lissa grabbed our arms and began to drag us back to camp.

"You don't want to say hi?" I asked Lissa.

"No! That's—no!" Lissa said, then sighed. "I'm terrified to say hi. I'd end up saying something stupid."

"I'm sure you'd be fine," I said. "Maybe you could tell him you liked his reel."

Lissa nervously chewed on one of her nails. "No, not today," she finally said. "Maybe next feis."

Fiona rolled her eyes *again*. "She's never going to talk to him," she told me. Then she laughed. "Hey, we're not identical, but we look enough alike. I could pretend to be you and talk to him?"

"Don't you dare!" Lissa said.

Fiona and I both laughed. "Okay, relax!" Fiona said.

We noticed Molly and Aunt Lydia returning to the camp. Molly had changed out of her solo dress into denim shorts and a T-shirt. Her eyes looked red.

"What's going on?" Fiona asked.

"Molly is going to sit this one out," Aunt Lydia said crisply.

I could tell Molly definitely wasn't happy, even though she wouldn't have to dance for the rest of the day.

Eighteen

At our next dance class I got to try out my new "poodle" socks (the twins told me that's what they were called) and ghillies. I didn't bother texting Yumi or Amber about how excited I was. I knew they wouldn't understand.

I felt like I was fitting in much better now—I wasn't that girl from out of town who kept wearing the wrong shoes to class. The ghillies were similar to my leather ballet slippers, but somehow they had the power to suddenly transform my feet. When I wore them I felt like I was really becoming an Irish dancer. I kept my legs crossed as I danced and my hands down at my sides. My years of ballet meant my posture was excellent, and I could easily make the Irish steps quick and clean. I didn't care what Amber thought—Irish dancing was keeping me sharp. I was sure that when I returned to ballet class, my jumps would be higher. My stamina was improving too.

At the end of the week Anna asked to speak to me after class.

"You are doing remarkably well," Anna told me when the other dancers had left the room.

"Thank you," I said.

"Have you thought about competing at the Rose City Feis? It's only three weeks away, but I think we can still send in a registration if you're interested."

"Yes!" I said. "I would love to compete at the feis!"

Anna smiled. "I thought you might say that. I filled out your registration form for you already. Just make sure your aunt sends it in right away, okay?"

"Okay," I said as I took the form. I glanced down and saw that she had filled in the dances I would be competing in—reel, light jig and *slip jig*!

"Really?" I said, looking up at Anna.

"You'll be learning your slip jig steps next class," Anna said. "You've earned it."

"Thank you!" I said.

* * *

I didn't want to let Anna down. I spent all of the next day practicing in the home studio.

"Geez, even Lissa and Fiona don't practice this much," Molly said from her favorite spot on the bottom step. She had a large hardcover book about tropical fish open on her lap. The twins were over at a friend's house. They had invited me to join them, but I wanted to practice. I only had three weeks until my very first feis.

"I just don't want to mess up," I told her.

"Like I did?" Molly asked.

"No, I didn't mean that," I said. "I've just never competed in anything before. I don't want to get up onstage and forget what I'm doing."

"I've done that before too! Many times! It's even more embarrassing than falling," Molly said.

"But your mom said you don't have to compete anymore, right? So that's good, isn't it?" While we talked I danced around the room, practicing my reel.

"Yeah, but she still makes me go to the stupid classes," Molly said.

"You really dislike dancing *that* much? But you're so good!"

"It's boring," Molly said.

I stopped and looked at her. "Well, maybe you need to have another chat with your mom."

"Yeah, maybe..." Molly said and went back to looking at her fish book.

Nineteen

I was a bit anxious about that evening's class. Anna had promised I would finally learn a slip jig. After we had done warm-up, reels and light jigs, Anna asked a girl named Cora to teach me her slip jig. It was similar to the one Molly had shown me, so I caught on quickly. It was beautiful. When I had mastered it, we returned to the classroom. It felt amazing to get in line with the other dancers. I danced my slip jig alongside Cora, and this time Anna looked pleased.

"Well done today," Anna told me as I took off my ghillies at the end of class. "Make sure your aunt sends off the registration for the feis as soon as possible."

"She already did!"

"Wonderful!" Anna said. "Keep up the hard work."

"Thank you," I said. Then suddenly I realized something. "But what am I going to wear?"

"Don't worry. The school has some rental dresses," Anna said. "I'll bring the ones I think might fit you to our next class, and you can pick one out, okay?"

"That sounds great. Thank you!"

* * *

My mom called that night, and I told her all about my new ghillies, learning the slip jig and the upcoming feis.

"I'm so happy you're having a good summer," she said.

I guessed my summer *was* turning out okay. Even if I hadn't heard from Yumi or Amber for over a week now.

"How about you? Still super busy?" I asked.

"Yes. I should be done by the last week of August."

"I wish you could come and see me dance at the feis," I said.

"I know. I am so sorry I can't be there. I've never missed a performance. I'll be thinking of you."

* * *

The night before the feis, my cousins put my hair in curlers. They used Molly's, since she wouldn't be competing.

"I will *not* miss soft spikes," Molly said with a laugh. "Actually, I don't think there's anything I'll miss about competing."

"Suit yourself, fish girl," Lissa teased.

Once they were done with the curlers, I stole a glance in the mirror. I looked ridiculous! The bright purple spikes were sticking out from my head at every possible angle. I'd seen my cousins with the curlers in their hair a few times now, but it was different to see myself wearing the crazy curlers.

"And I have to sleep with these in?" I asked.

"It's not that bad," Fiona said as she looked in the mirror and adjusted a few of hers. "They're called *soft* spikes for a reason—they're soft!"

"They're still not that great to sleep in," Molly said to me. "Good luck."

The curlers ended up not being *that* bad. The main thing that kept me awake was thinking about being onstage the next day. Even so, I woke up early to get ready. I asked Molly to help me take the curlers out in the morning. I had never had curly hair before.

I stood in front of the mirror and watched as Molly took out the first curler. The hair sprung right back up to my scalp.

"It's so short!" I gasped.

"Don't worry—the curls will relax a bit. And I'll separate them for you," Molly said.

She continued her work, unrolling and separating the pieces of hair into smaller strands. By the time she was done I had a curly mass of hair that was at least five inches shorter than usual—the curls were bouncing above my shoulders!

Fiona and Lissa peeked in the bathroom door that had been left ajar.

"Oooh, looking good!" Lissa said.

"C'mon, girls, time to leave!" Aunt Lydia called to us.

I looked through my backpack to be sure I had everything and then grabbed the garment bag that held the solo dress I had borrowed from the school. I couldn't wait to put it on at the feis—with my socks and ghillies and my hair in curls!

The feis was at the local university recreation center, so we didn't have far to drive. We found a spot to set up our camp and located all of our stages. I did some warm-ups with the twins—jogging on the spot, points, point hop backs, cuts and then some stretching.

"You should probably get changed now. Beginner dances might be starting soon," Fiona said. The twins had already changed into their school dresses and were about to head over to their two-hand-reel stage.

I nodded and took my garment bag to the girls' dressing room. Molly came with me to help.

"It feels so nice to *not* have to worry about dancing!" Molly said as we entered the dressing room. "How are you feeling? Nervous? Excited? Wishing you never signed up for this?"

"A bit of the first two," I said. "Not so much the last one."

I quickly slipped off my street clothes and pulled on the solo dress. It was a sparkling blue, with pink and yellow sequins in Celtic knot designs—much fancier than any of my ballet costumes.

"*Now* you look like an Irish dancer!" Molly said as she zipped me up and made sure everything was in its proper place.

"I'm starting to get more nervous now," I said, wringing my hands, which suddenly felt very sweaty. This wasn't a typical dance performance—I wouldn't be onstage performing the same dance as the rest of my ballet class. I would be dancing at the same time as a dancer I had never met before, and I'd be the only one dancing my steps—I couldn't look to a fellow dancer for help if I forgot my next move. I'd never even done a solo in ballet before.

"Oh, they have a mirror!" Molly said and dragged me over to the full-length mirror set up in the dressing room. "Check it out!"

I gasped. I really did look like an Irish dancer, from head to toe. I felt a swarm of butterflies begin to flutter in my stomach.

"Oh! I promised my mom a selfie," I said. I grabbed my phone from my bag.

I snapped a quick mirror pic and texted it to my mom. I was about to put my phone away but decided to send the picture to Yumi too. And to

Amber. Then I shut my phone off and put it back in my bag.

"C'mon. Let's go," Molly said.

As we walked over to the first stage I spotted Thomas coming toward us. He was just a few steps away when he finally noticed me—and stopped dead in his tracks.

"Natalie?" he said, taking in my sparkly dress and head of curls. "You look amazing! No one will know you're secretly a ballerina!" He winked.

I tried not to show how pleased I was by his words. I needed to concentrate!

Twenty

"Natalie's dancing on stage two in a few minutes," Molly told Thomas. "You should stick around and watch!"

"Wouldn't miss it," Thomas said.

I glared at Molly. What was she doing? Trying to make me even *more* nervous?

There were still two dances ahead of mine, but Molly said it would be best for me to just wait at the stage, as sometimes it was hard to tell how much time each age group would take.

I saw a few other girls and one boy about my age waiting around the stage too. The girls all had beautiful sparkly dresses and curly hair. Some of them even had rhinestone-encrusted tiaras perched in their curls.

I felt a bit awkward waiting with Molly and Thomas. Molly kept glancing from Thomas to me and back again, a huge grin on her freckled face.

"Are you nervous?" Thomas asked me.

"Yeah, a little...I mean...a lot," I said, wringing my sweaty hands again.

"I still get nervous," Thomas said with a smile.

"How many competitions have you been to?" I asked him.

"Um...hundreds?" Thomas said. "My mom started me really young. At my first feis I did the Tir na Nog."

I couldn't help but imagine how cute that would have been.

"And you still get nervous?" I asked.

"Yeah, but that's part of the fun—the adrenaline," he said.

I nodded. "Yeah, I guess. Sometimes I feel that way during ballet recitals. And then suddenly I can kick higher than I've ever kicked before!"

"Yeah, exactly!" Thomas said.

My turn was coming up soon. The other dancers began to find seats in the waiting area. I followed them. Finally, our judge, a middle-aged man wearing a suit, arrived and took his seat at the table in front of the stage. I walked with the other dancers onto the stage. I was paired with a girl wearing a red-and-gold solo dress. We would be the third to dance. The musician started playing his accordion. My heart began to race.

I watched the first two girls step forward and start their reels. They were both beginners and had beginner reels like my own, but they danced so well! They looked confident, not nervous at all. They finished, bowed to the judge and then to the musician. The next two girls began to dance.

As the girls finished their second step on their left side, I stepped forward, and the girl next to me followed. The dancers bowed. We pointed our right feet, rose onto our tiptoes and began to dance. I concentrated on my steps, on keeping my legs and ankles crossed, on pointing my feet and keeping my arms straight at my sides. Before I knew it, my steps were done and I was bowing. I barely remembered a thing. I went back to my spot in line and watched the last few pairings dance their reels, my heart racing even faster. The last pair finished dancing and the musician ended his song. We all pointed our right feet and bowed to the judge once more before leaving the stage.

Aunt Lydia, all three of my cousins and Thomas were waiting by the stage.

"Great job, Natalie!" Fiona said.

"One down, two to go!" Molly said.

"Fiona and I have to go change into our solo dresses now, but we'll try to catch the rest of your dances too!" Lissa said before running off with Fiona.

"You were wonderful," Aunt Lydia said. "I'm so happy you had the opportunity to dance this summer."

"Thank you for bringing me to classes and everything," I said.

"It was my pleasure," Aunt Lydia said. "I should probably go help the girls get changed."

Aunt Lydia left with Molly, but not before glancing at Thomas with a small smile on her face. Molly looked over her shoulder at me and grinned. My face burned.

"Yeah, like the others said, great job!" said Thomas.

"Well, I had a good teacher!" I said, hoping Thomas knew I was referring to him.

Thomas laughed. "I guess so," he said. "Well, I better go check and see when my next dance is. Want to come with me?"

"Yeah, sure," I said.

The next hour passed in a blur as I went from stage to stage—watching Thomas dance, watching the twins dance and dancing my own light jig. I checked the results board with Molly to see if I had placed in the reel, but no luck. Right before my slip jig was about to begin, I found out I hadn't placed in my light jig either.

"Don't worry about it! *This* is your dance," Molly whispered to me. "You can do this! Think *gold medal.*"

I laughed and shooed her away. As we lined up onstage I realized I would be dancing last— this time with a girl wearing a green-and-black dress. I couldn't see Thomas in the audience. I was a little disappointed that he'd seen my reel and light jig but would miss my slip jig. My heart was racing again, but I kept telling myself how the slip jig reminded me of a butterfly—quick, graceful, beautiful. I tried to focus on those words. *Quick. Graceful. Beautiful.* Just before I stepped forward, I saw Thomas walk up behind Molly.

He smiled and waved at me. I smiled back, rose onto my toes and began the dance I had wanted to dance all summer long.

Twenty-One

D ancing my slip jig felt wonderful. I was quick. I was graceful. I felt beautiful. After the last bow I exited the stage and began to walk over to my audience. And there was my mom! When did she get here?

"Mom!" I said, running into her outstretched arms. I felt a little embarrassed to be hugging my mom in front of Thomas, but I hadn't realized until that moment how much I had missed her.

"You were brilliant!" my mom said as she took a step back to get a good look at me in my solo dress. "You certainly don't look like a ballerina today!"

"That was slip jig. It's my favorite Irish dance," I said. "But I don't want to stop ballet classes!" I quickly added.

"I didn't think you would!" my mom said.

"But maybe we could help you find an Irish-dance school in Toronto?" Aunt Lydia suggested.

I looked from Aunt Lydia to my mom.

"If Natalie would like to, I don't see why not," she said.

"Really?" I asked.

"I got a promotion. We should be able to afford it," my mom said with a smile.

"That's amazing, Mom! Congrats! And thank you!" I said and gave her another hug. "How did you get here? I thought you weren't going to be done for another week!"

My mom told me she had managed to wrap up her work assignment early and wanted to surprise me. She had phoned Aunt Lydia for directions. As I listened, I realized Thomas had disappeared. He probably had a dance coming up.

After my mom had taken photos of me in my solo dress, I went to the dressing room to change. As I riffled through my bag, I found my phone. I turned it on. There were three messages, one from my mom, telling me I looked beautiful, and one from Yumi:

Wowzers! That's an Irish-dancing dress? So much bling! You look amazing, Natalie! Pinkies!

And one from Amber:

Wow, so you really have turned into an Irish dancer. Guess you don't have to worry about what class you're in if you don't even come back to ballet.

I frowned. What was her problem with me Irish dancing? I was going to ignore her. But then I thought, why not just *ask* her what her deal was?

I'll be coming back to ballet. Trust me, I miss it. I miss you. I miss Yumi. Heck, I even miss Madame Lebrun. I thought this summer would be awful without you guys and ballet. But I got to try something new and I'm glad I did. I don't understand why you're being so mean. I miss you. More than ballet.

I took a deep breath and hit *Send.* I waited. Nothing. I chucked my phone back into my bag. I had just finished changing when I heard the familiar *ding* of my phone.

Sorry. About…everything. I mean, you're already good at ballet, and now you're also an Irish dancer? I just felt like you were abandoning your ballet friends. But then you're not even leaving ballet. You're probably going to come back and not even miss a beat, while I've been slaving away with Madame Lebrun all summer. It's not fair.

Hey, it wasn't my choice to leave ballet for an entire summer. To leave you.

I know. I'm sorry. Class has been really hard this summer. And you're usually my personal cheerleader. I've missed you.

I miss you too. And I'll be coming home very soon. I'll see you in class in Sept.

As long as I don't get moved down a class. See you soon, Nat.

As if that would ever happen. But I knew what it felt like to be worried about falling behind. I sent her one last text.

I'll see you IN CLASS. XOXOX

Twenty-Two

I found Molly and my mom waiting at the results board. Molly was jumping up and down.

"*Look*! There you are! Number 398!" Molly said, pointing to my number on the results board.

"Are you sure? Is that right?" I asked.

"Yes!" Molly exclaimed. "You won a gold medal!"

"Gold!" my mom said. "Congratulations, Natalie!"

Molly told me I had to check in with one of the officials at the desk. I showed them my number and they had me sign a paper. Then they gave me my medal! It had a green ribbon, and on the medal itself were the words *Rose City Feis* in the center and a border of tiny gold roses.

I snapped a picture and sent it to Yumi. And then I also sent it to Amber. I hoped she wouldn't think I was rubbing it in her face. I hoped she would be happy for me, now that we had made up.

I ate lunch with my mom while we waited for Fiona's and Lissa's final dances. They both ended up getting silver medals—Lissa in hornpipe and Fiona in slip jig. I looked for Thomas but didn't see him anywhere. As we got ready to leave, I did one more scan.

"Looking for your *boyfriend*?" Molly asked.

"No!" I said.

My mom glanced at me.

"She's kidding!" I said. I spotted Thomas walking over to us.

"Hi," he said shyly. "Can I talk to you? Before you go?"

"Um...sure," I said.

"Over...somewhere," he said, sounding a little awkward.

"We get it," Aunt Lydia said and nudged my mom and the girls to leave Thomas and me alone.

"Who's that?" I heard my mom ask as she walked off with them.

"So that's your mom," Thomas said with a nervous laugh.

"Yeah, she finished her work thing early. I guess I get to go home now," I said.

"I just...wanted to say goodbye before you left," he said. "And tell you I'm really happy you got that gold medal for your slip jig. I know how hard you worked for it."

"Thanks," I said, unsure of what else to say.

"Here," he said, passing me a folded piece of paper. "My phone number...so, you know, we can keep in touch. And maybe we'll see each other at some competitions."

"Thanks," I said, unable to control the huge smile spreading across my face. "I hope so!"

Twenty-Three

I met up with everyone in the parking lot. My cousins started teasing me right away. I was thankful I could drive back to their house in my mom's car.

But as soon as we got in the car, my mom looked at me with her Serious Mom Face.

"Is he *really* your boyfriend like Molly says?" she asked.

"No!" I said. "He's just my friend. Who happens to be a boy. He's in our Irish-dance class. He just wanted to say goodbye before I left."

"Why haven't you ever mentioned him before?"

I shrugged. "I didn't think it was a big deal. Because he's *not* my boyfriend."

My mom was still wearing her Serious Mom Face but kept her eyes on the road.

"I *am* old enough to have a boyfriend," I mumbled.

"I know you are," my mom said. "But it doesn't mean I have to like it!"

"But he's *not* my boyfriend," I repeated.

My mom finally sighed and smiled a tiny smile. "Well, he seems like a nice young man."

*　*　*

After meeting up with Uncle Nolan we decided we should all go out for a big family dinner. It ended up being a farewell dinner too, since I was going home with my mom the next morning.

"I can't thank you enough for letting Natalie stay with you this summer," my mom said.

"It was our pleasure," said Aunt Lydia as we seated ourselves around the big table in the middle of the restaurant. "Maybe we should plan to all get together at Christmas."

"Yeah!" I said at the same time as my cousins. I smiled.

My mom nodded. "That would be great."

"Are you excited to go back to ballet?" Molly asked, passing me a menu.

"Yeah, I am," I said. "But I wouldn't mind keeping up with Irish dancing."

"I'm sure we can find a class nearby," said my mom. "It made me so happy watching you dance today!" She looked over at my aunt and uncle. "Isn't it wonderful seeing the joy dance can bring?"

Aunt Lydia glanced at Molly. "It certainly is," she said.

* * *

When we got back from dinner I went upstairs to pack.

Molly came into the room and threw herself onto her bed, face down.

"Are you okay?" I asked. I was sitting on the floor, trying to get all my clothes to fit in my suitcase.

Molly rolled over. "I just told my mom I want to quit dancing. I don't even want to go to the stupid classes anymore."

"And?" I asked.

"She said okay," Molly said. "I was so surprised! She looked a bit sad but said she understood and just wants me to be happy."

"So, how do you feel?" I asked.

"Happy. Relieved. Free!" Molly said, now sitting up and smiling.

"So now you'll have lots of time for your fish hobby. Are you going to help your dad in the store more?"

"Actually, I was thinking about trying out for soccer," Molly said. "I've always wanted to play on the school team."

"That's great! Trying new things can be fun," I said. I smiled as I picked up my ghillies and packed them in my suitcase, right next to my ballet slippers.

Much of Elizabeth J.M. Walker's childhood and teen years were spent in dance classes, which explains why so much dancing finds its way into her books and stories. She currently volunteers with a local dance theater company, where she helps plan productions, writes scripts and choreographs dances. She lives in Windsor, Ontario, with her husband and their creatures: two cats and a dog. For more information, visit www.elizabethjmwalker.com.